Claire Freedman has written over 50 picture books for children, including many international bestsellers. Claire enjoyed writing this ballerina story and indulging her sparkly pink girly side!

Lorna Brown studied fine art painting in college and works as an artist and illustrator from her cottage in Somerset, England. Lorna also works as an animal therapist, so she has the perfect balance between art and her love of animals and the outdoors!

Sandy Creek
NEW YORK

An Imprint of Sterling Publishing
387 Park Avenue South
New York, NY 10016

Text © 2012 by Parragon Books Ltd
Illustrations © 2012 by Parragon Books Ltd

This 2013 edition published by Sandy Creek.

ISBN 978-1-4351-4918-2

Manufactured in Shenzhen, China
Lot #: 2 4 6 8 10 9 7 5 3 1

06/13

The Butterfly Ballerina

Sandy Creek
NEW YORK

Isabella Ballerina loved ballet.

She liked twirling around
in her pretty leotard.
She loved wearing her
satin ballet shoes.

Best of all, she liked going to Madame Colette's Ballet School. "Come, *mes petites!*" said Madame Colette—who was French and had once been a real ballerina.

"Let us begin by warming up!"

The girls began their bending
and stretching exercises.

"Now, let us practice our ballet positions!"
said Madame Colette, clapping her hands, as
Ms. Robin played a beautiful tune on the piano.

"*Non, non*, Isabella!" cried Madame Colette. "You are pointing the wrong foot again!"

"Oops, sorry!" Isabella said.
"I'm always getting my left
and right mixed up!"

Isabella concentrated very hard, and the rest of the lesson went really well. She only turned the wrong way twice!

"*Bien!* Good!" said Madame Colette. "Wonderful pirouette, Isabella! Now, I have exciting news to announce!"

Madame Colette told the girls that they would
be putting on their very first ballet show.
"We will dance the Butterfly Ballet!" she said.
"This ballet is set in a beautiful flower garden.

I will choose girls to
play raindrop butterflies,

girls to be rainbow butterflies,

and one girl to dance the
beautiful sunshine butterfly!"

Back home, Isabella told Mom all about the ballet. "Madame Colette says my ballet is getting better," she said.

"I just wish I could remember my left from my right!"

"This might help my little Butterfly Ballerina!" Mom smiled. She gave Isabella a beautiful butterfly bracelet.

"Wear it on your right wrist; then you'll always be able to tell which way is right," Mom told Isabella.

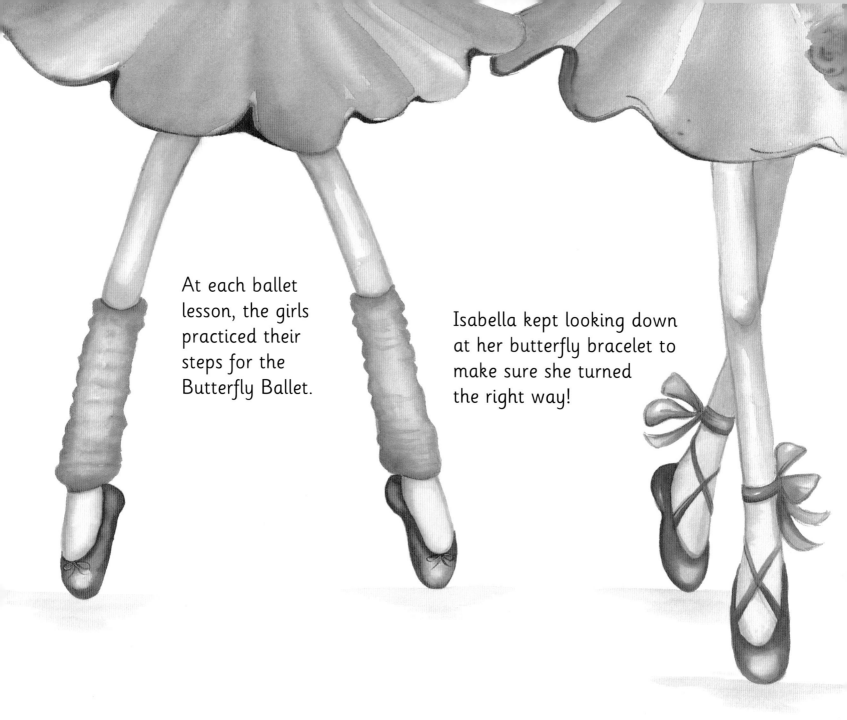

At each ballet lesson, the girls practiced their steps for the Butterfly Ballet.

Isabella kept looking down at her butterfly bracelet to make sure she turned the right way!

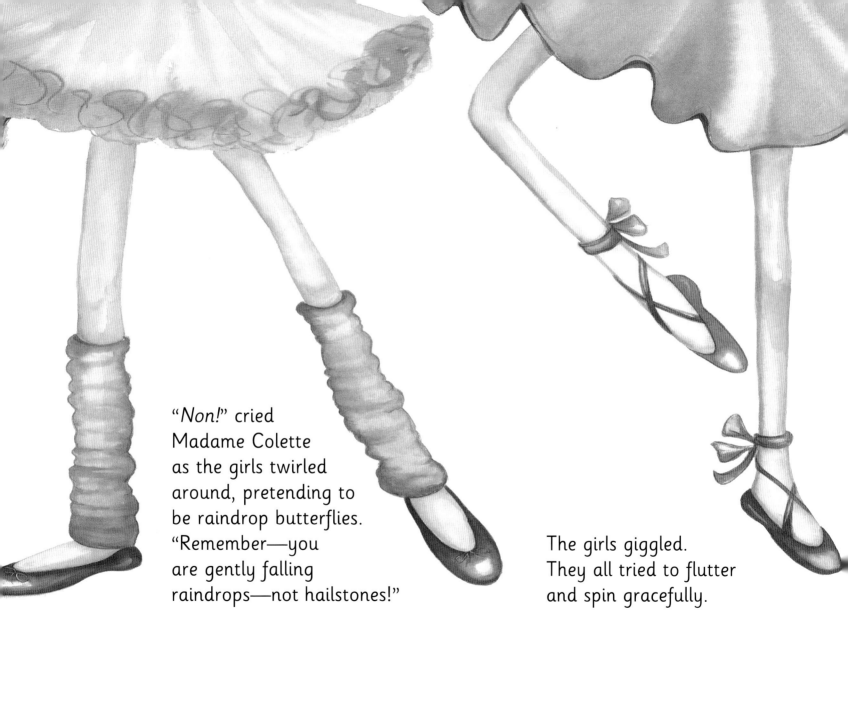

"*Non!*" cried Madame Colette as the girls twirled around, pretending to be raindrop butterflies. "Remember—you are gently falling raindrops—not hailstones!"

The girls giggled. They all tried to flutter and spin gracefully.

Finally the decision time came and Madame Colette told the girls, one by one, if they were going to be a raindrop or rainbow butterfly.

Soon only Isabella was left. "Oh no!" she thought. "I hope Madame Colette isn't leaving me out of the ballet because she's worried I might get my left and right mixed up!"

"Isabella, *ma petite!*" said Madame Colette. "You shall play the sunshine butterfly. As you twirl so beautifully, you will dance the final pirouette!"

Isabella just hoped she would turn the right way!

The week before the show, Isabella practiced her pirouettes everywhere! She twirled in the yard ...

in her bedroom ...

and at the park with
her best friend, Hannah.

On the night of the big show, all the girls dressed in gorgeous tutus and delicate, shimmering butterfly wings. They tied matching ribbons in each other's hair. "Now we feel like real butterflies!" they giggled to each other.

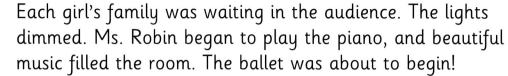

Each girl's family was waiting in the audience. The lights dimmed. Ms. Robin began to play the piano, and beautiful music filled the room. The ballet was about to begin!

Out danced the raindrop butterflies, flitting gracefully from flower to flower. Their sparkly costumes twinkled in the soft lights.

Next, the colorful rainbow butterflies danced out, linking arms before a beautiful arching rainbow.

At last it was Isabella's
turn to dance.
Nervously, she touched
her butterfly bracelet.

Then she stepped
lightly onto the stage.

She fluttered to the middle,
took a deep breath, and
twirled the most perfect
pirouette she had ever twirled!

The girls joined Isabella on stage, and they all curtsied to the final tinkling notes of the music. Isabella smiled and touched her beautiful bracelet.

"Oops!" she giggled. She had curtsied with the wrong foot forward, but it didn't matter one little bit.

She would always be Isabella, Butterfly Ballerina!